TAKE TURNS

DISCARD

Taking turns
is the right thing to do,
whether you're a little bear
or a kid like you!

Mike Berenstain

Based on the characters created by
Stan and Jan Berenstain

An Imprint of HarperCollinsPublishers

HarperFestival is an imprint of HarperCollins Publishers.
The Berenstain Bears Take Turns
Copyright © 2022 by Berenstain Publishing, Inc. All rights reserved. Printed in the United States of America.
No part of this book may be used or reproduced in any manner whatsoever without written permission except in the case
of brief quotations embodied in critical articles and reviews. For information address HarperCollins Children's Books,
a division of HarperCollins Publishers, 195 Broadway, New York, NY 10007. www.harpercollinschildrens.com
Library of Congress Control Number: 2021942560 ISBN 978-0-06-302433-5
21 22 23 24 25 CWM 10 9 8 7 6 5 4 3 2 1 ❖ First Edition

Brother, Sister, and little Honey were a great team.
They were good at baseball, with Brother usually pitching,
Sister fielding, and Honey catching while they all took
turns at bat.

The three cubs teamed up for board games, too.
Their favorite was Bearopoly.

Sister was usually the banker—
she was good at math.

Brother always tried to buy up
parcels of real estate.

Honey, on the other hand,
was a builder. She built lots and
lots of houses and hotels.
Honey usually won.

But the cubs' best teamwork came from playing "pretend" games—like pretending they were Robin Hood and his Merry Bears, or Peter Pan and the Lost Bears, or Beary Potter.

All three cubs had lots of fun with these games. They really got into their roles, and their games could last all day, or even all week. The only problem was they didn't always agree about their roles. Brother usually wanted to be the brave (and sensitive) hero. Sister usually wanted to be the beautiful (and brave) princess.

Unfortunately, that usually left Honey as the villain—the
Sheriff of Nottingbear, or Captain Hook, or Lord Grizzlymort.

After a while, Honey got fed up with being the villain. One day, she put her little foot down.

"Let's play Robin Hood," said Brother. "I'll be Robin Hood. Okay?"

"Okay," said Sister. "I'll be Maid Bearian."

"Fine," said Brother. "Honey, you can be the Sheriff of Nottingbear."

"Nope!" said Honey, folding her arms. "Don't wanna be the bad guy!"

Brother and Sister were annoyed.

"But you're always the bad guy!" said Brother.

"Don't wanna be the bad guy!" said Honey firmly.

Brother and Sister didn't know what to do. Someone had to be the bad guy or they couldn't play. What's Robin Hood without a bad guy? But Honey wouldn't budge. She just stood there with her arms folded. Finally, Brother gave in.

"Okay," he said, "you can be Maid Bearian."

"Wait a minute!" said Sister. "I don't want to be the bad guy, either!"

"Well, neither do I," said Brother.

"Me, neither!" said Honey, arms still firmly folded.

"Okay! Okay!" said Brother. "You win. *I'll* be the Sheriff of Nottingbear."

So the three cubs played Robin Hood with Brother as the villain. It wasn't so bad. He got to do a lot of sneering and haughty laughing.

But, in the end, he had to lose the big sword fight and give in to Robin Hood and Maid Bearian.

The next day, the cubs decided to play another pretend game.

"How about Peter Pan?" asked Brother. "I'll be Peter, okay?"

"Okay," said Sister. "I'll be Wendy."

"Fine," said Brother. "Honey, you can be Captain Hook."

"Nope!" said Honey, folding her arms again. "Don't wanna be the bad guy!"

Brother and Sister were even more annoyed. Letting Honey have her own way with Robin Hood just seemed to have made things worse. Now she was even more stubborn than before.

"Don't wanna be the bad guy!" was all they could get out of her.

"What's all that commotion coming from the
family room?" wondered Papa as he sipped his
coffee in the kitchen.

"Don't know," said Mama, reading the paper.
"Sounds like the cubs."

Mama and Papa investigated.

They found the cubs yelling at each other, with Brother and Sister waving their arms while Honey stood there with her arms folded.

"What's going on here?" shouted Papa, trying to be heard. But the cubs just went on yelling.

Finally, Mama put her fingers to her mouth and whistled really *loud*.

TWE-E-ET!

That got everyone's attention.

"Thank you, Mama," said Papa. "Now, what's going on?"

The cubs all started talking at once. Papa and Mama got the basic idea right away.

"Hasn't anyone here heard of something called 'taking turns'?" asked Papa.

The cubs were embarrassed. Of course they'd heard of "taking turns." It just hadn't occurred to them.

"I think you'll find a little turn-taking will solve your problem quite nicely," said Mama as she and Papa went back to their coffee.

And it did.

From then on, Brother, Sister, and Honey took turns playing different roles. It was much more fair and prevented squabbles.

It also turned out to be much more fun. They hadn't realized playing the same roles over and over again was boring. The turn-taking system made things more interesting.

In the cubs' next game, Brother was
Beary Potter, Honey was Hermione,
and Sister was Lord Grizzlymort.

"Mwa-ha-ha!" Sister laughed wickedly. "I am Lord Grizzlymort, the all-powerful!"

Beary Potter and Hermione may win out in the end, but Lord Grizzlymort is a much juicer role!